# Always Alone

This book has been donated by a client who has found it inspirational and wishes to share it with others. You are welcome to borrow this book for **4 WEEKS BUT PLEASE RETURN IT**. Please make sure you book it out and back in. THANKS.

Revival
PO Box 4157
TROWBRIDGE
Wiltshire
BA14 4AW

Tel: 01225 757568

# Always Alone

❈

*Alex Benett*

iUniverse, Inc.
New York  Lincoln  Shanghai

## Always Alone

Copyright © 2005 by Alex Bennett

All rights reserved. No part of this book may be used or reproduced by any means, graphic, electronic, or mechanical, including photocopying, recording, taping or by any information storage retrieval system without the written permission of the publisher except in the case of brief quotations embodied in critical articles and reviews.

iUniverse books may be ordered through booksellers or by contacting:

iUniverse
2021 Pine Lake Road, Suite 100
Lincoln, NE 68512
www.iuniverse.com
1-800-Authors (1-800-288-4677)

ISBN: 0-595-34988-9

Printed in the United States of America

# *Chapter One (Intro)*

My name is Alex and I am twenty-four years old. Things I would say are very good for me right now. I finally achieved my goals in life. I have a family a house and a slew of rescued animals. To get to where I am now was definitely my biggest challenge. I was born in a really small town and grew up in a housing project with. My mother and my brother Mike. When you are born and raised in a place like that you are most likely going to stay in a place like that. It is much harder for someone to start with absolutely nothing and make it then someone who has stable ground to stand on.

    My mother and father are divorced. They got divorced when I was very young. I have no memory of them together. My older brother Mike who is six years older then me does but never talks about it. I guess it wasn't so great so I never ask. I like to imagine at some point in time we were a happy normal family. My mother is an alcoholic. She drinks just about every day as long as she can afford it. She is a very high strung person who is always the life of the party. On days she is sober or alone she is a whole different person. She is a very depressed and hurt woman and spends a lot of time having a pity party for herself and the way she grew up.

    Her real mother left her with her aunt when she was five. She says she can remember standing at the screen door crying. She said she would sit for hours at a time on them steps hoping that one day she would return to get her. She never came back for her. So her Aunt and uncle who had three kids of their own have raised her. They were also alcoholics and they seemed to always take everything out on her with bad beatings and endless punishments of being locked in the attic. She heard them argue a lot about having to take her in and how it was a real strain on their family. I have heard more stories then I would have liked to but when she got drunk alone she would just sit and tell anyone who would listen. Which was either me or my brother? I don't know how someone who was practically tortured by alcoholics would grow up to be one.

My father who also likes to party never really had time for us. His mother would always come over and help us out with food or whatever it was we needed. Of course she was as poor as the next guy but anything she had she would give. I never even really remember ever seeing him until I was about six when my mom took him to court for child support and they granted him with every other weekend visits. My mom made us go because if she didn't send us he didn't have to send the check. I was so scared and nervous about being around him that my grandmother went with us for every weekend visit and slept on the couch at his house. That was great for him though he could still go out at night. He was always very nice to us and never hit us but I didn't know him and at the time I couldn't understand that if he was my dad where has he been?

I lived in a typical housing project with my mother since I was born. I always had lots of friends. All of us kids that lived there were all there for the same reason. Our parents never did anything with their lives. We all raised each other. My mother was never home. She worked during the day and was out drinking just about every night. My brother was always told to keep an eye on me. But he was six years older then me and wanted to be out with his friends so I spent a lot of time alone. I can remember being six years old home alone. I would put a blanket over the kitchen table and make a fort and hide in there with my dog Charlie until someone came home. I had to stay in the kitchen because my mother never allowed Charlie to go anywhere in the house but the kitchen. If I had got caught with

Charlie in my bedroom or something I would have gotten a really good beating and that would probably be the last I saw of Charlie. I couldn't let that happen Charlie was the only thing that made me feel safe all alone in the house. He was a very big strong dog that would intimidate anyone that came through the door. He was all I had and I think he knew it.

When my mother would be home in the mornings because she called out of work a lot. I always knew it would be a bad day. I was not aloud to make noise and she always told me to get out of the house and go play that she was trying to sleep and she didn't feel very well. Basically she was hung over and didn't want me in the house only to use the bathroom. There were days I would sit outside in the woods next to my house starving and cold but just too scared to go home. I hated when she was home. One time I was about six and me and my friend were out back playing in my yard while my mother was in the house sleeping and we both had to use the bathroom. My friend asked to use my bathroom and I was too ashamed to say no so I quick snuck us in. While we were in the bathroom my mother came in furious and threw my friend out and grabbed me off the toilet and beat me so bad. I had to sit in my room the rest of the day which meant I didn't eat because she never made anything for us. The beating and the punishment hurt me a lot but I was more ashamed and embarrassed that my friend had to see it. I didn't want everyone to know how bad it was at home. Mike would always tell me to just get over it and not to let her break me down that one day I would be older and could get out of here. I'm so glad Mike was always there for me I don't know how I would have gotten through one day without him.

My brother always helped me out when he was home but he was out a lot with his friends and I really don't blame him. Like at two o'clock in the morning on a school night when she would bring all of her friends home from the bar. They would play the radio so loud that I would wake up and couldn't sleep. I would go wake him up and he would go downstairs and fight with her about being quiet for me. When she was drunk and in front of her friends she had the happy go lucky attitude and would laugh at him and act like it was no big deal. She made it seem as though we were raining on her parade. She would always say well now that you're up you should stay up and hang with me and my friends. He would say about us having school tomorrow and she would always say forget school it's useless anyway just stay home. But me and Mike never did that school was much easier then dealing with her all hung over the next day. He also would always fight with her about leaving me home alone all the time when I was so young in a bad neighbor hood. She would say Alex is a tough kid she is fine. The truth was I wasn't very fine. The nights seemed as though they would never end and minutes ticked by like hours. The fear of being alone in the case of an emergency is something most kids never have to worry about but was something I had to deal with every day.

I would call my grandmother a lot when she was gone and she would sit on the phone with me when I was scared. She didn't have a car so it made it impossible for her to get over there every time I was alone. I would ask her to please not hang up if she needed to use the bathroom I would just sit on hold. Most nights our calls ended by me falling asleep on the other end of the phone. She had a friend that lived a couple of doors down from us and my grandmother would call her and send me over to get a few sandwiches for me and my brother. I hated doing that it was so embarrassing. I wanted to cry every time I had to do that. When my mother found out, she was doing that she started sending us around the neighborhood with a note asking people for bread or cheese she even made us do that for her cigarettes. I would beg for her not to make me do this every day but it was do it or get in big trouble so I would go furious with tears in my eyes. It got to the point nobody would give us anything anymore. She would get so pissed at the neighbors but would still send us every day I think just to get on the neighbors nerves. She would sit in her bedroom window and watch us go to their houses so that we couldn't lie and just saying that they said no. She never gave a shit what that was doing to me and Mike. This went on for about a year until finally a few of the neighbors confronted her and told her to stop sending us around to do her begging. She was so pissed and I think a little embarrassed she never told me and Mike why she stopped sending us. We found out through my grandmother and we all agreed she got what she deserved.

By the time I was about eight or nine I was home alone so often that my grandmother told my mom the neighbors were going to call children and youth services. They could see me every night in the kitchen through our sliding glass doors sitting under the table with a flashlight lit. They also said they witnessed numerous accounts when I was being beaten. They also saw her take me outside and pour hot sauce down my throat for calling her a drunk. I almost choked to death and about ten neighbors were out front at a barbecue and I guess finally saw enough. So my mom asked my grandmother to move in with us for a while until she could get back control of herself and her life. That of course never happened but having my grandmother around was really nice. I had breakfast every morning and dinner every night. She made me feel as though I had a mother around. She did our laundry and cleaned the house. Our house usually always had empty bottles everywhere and smelled of alcohol and vomit. I usually did all the cleaning and laundry I mean somebody had to do it. I sometimes got very overwhelmed with all the chores and homework so with my grandmother around I had much more time to just be with my friends and more importantly just be a kid.

My mother of course did not like her around so much. I never could figure out why. She would say things like she doesn't do the dishes well. She leaves food spots on the silverware. The longer my grandmother was there the more my mother kept picking at her. My mother would say you can go home now we don't need you here anymore but my grandmother always kissed her ass and bit her tongue because she knew when she walked out that would leave me overwhelmed with chores and alone again. I would beg my grandmother please don't leave me here alone again. She would always tell me she could only stay as long as my mother allowed her to and there was only so much she could do or say to convince her that I needed her there. I could tell she was just afraid as I was to leave me there. She managed to stay with us for a whole year but my mother made her go. My mother was a very selfish and jealous person and could see how much we loved my grandmother. That made her furious. She was our mother and she expected us to love her more then anything no matter what she did. One thing my mother never figured out is we loved our grandmother so much because she gave us so much love. I'll never forget the day she left. I cried so hard up in my room. I didn't want her to go. I felt like she had just gotten there. I never let my mother see how badly she hurt me because she loved that kind of stuff it made her feel powerful and in control.

## Chapter Two

After my grandmother left things went straight back down hill. The night my grandmother left my mom of course went out on one of her all night drinking trips. That morning I got up for school and found her in the bathroom on the floor. There was vomit everywhere in the tub, on the floor, in the toilet and in the sink. She lifted her head and asked me to help her to bed. I laid her in her bed and put a trash can next to her. She asked me if I could stay home from school that day to clean the house. She also told me that when her boss called to please tell him she was deathly sick and wouldn't be coming in today. I of course said yes. I was furious inside though. I cleaned the whole house up because she had wrecked the whole house. By the time her boss called I was so mad and worked up from cleaning for two hours I told her boss she was sick and wouldn't be in because she went out all night drinking and got sick all over the house and made me clean it up. Her boss said I am so sorry honey but will you give your mom a message for me. I said sure. She told me to tell her she was fired and they would mail her last check that they didn't want her coming back up there. I didn't tell my mother until later that night and no matter how much trouble I was going to get in I finally had the guts to stand up to her and let her see that I had a mind of my own and was not happy with the way she chose for us all to live.

   She was sitting at the kitchen table that night when I told her and I'll never forget her face. She Jumped up and was just stunned and kept saying over and over again that I better be making it up or I would be really sorry. I kept reassuring her that I was not lying and she could call her old work in the morning and they could tell her for their selves. She screamed for me to get out of her face that she couldn't even stand the sight of me. She said if I come over there I will probably beat the shit out of you and wont be able to stop. I ran out of the house because that I definitely did believe. By the time I got home that night she of course was gone. Over the next couple of weeks things got really bad because she had no job she was home every day. She could no longer afford the bar every night she lived off of our child support checks. She would make me walk to the local bar with her and sit under the bar on the ledge where you put your feet to rest. She would drink a couple of vodka and orange juices while I just sat there as if I were invisible. She would tell me I had to be really quiet or I would get in trouble. Because if I bothered anyone or made too much noise we would get kicked out. I remember sitting there sometimes for hours not saying a word. Then she would get take out beer to take home because drinks at the bar cost a lot. She would then sit at home and drink till she passed out. She would cry for hours some nights just sitting next to the radio. Some nights while she was sitting there and I would walk past she would spin her head around with this evil look on her face and yell look at me you did this to me. You kids are so ungrateful and just want to bring me down. She always claimed that she gave up her life for us kids and that maybe she should have just dropped us off like her mother dropped her off. She started calling her friend in Florida a lot. They would talk for hours. She seemed to be getting really depressed at the time. She talked about us all just getting up and leaving. Starting over somewhere new. She said it was this atmosphere around here and the people in it that caused her to get so depressed and drink so much. It was funny how from night to night she would change. Some nights she would tell us how she loved us and other nights we seemed to be the enemy.

I got home from school a little late that day and nobody was home. Which wasn't unusual being it was the second week in the month. That was when the support checks came. So I looked around the house and noticed that all her stuff was gone off of her vanity. I ran over to the closet and sure enough her clothes were gone too. I ran downstairs to call my grandmother and I saw a note on the kitchen table that said kids I'm really sorry but I will call your grandmother to come stay with you two as soon as I get a chance. Gary is in charge until she can make it over. I am on my way to Florida. My friend got me a job and I really need this right now. I want to clean my act up. I love you both. Mom. I couldn't believe it. How could you do this to your kids? Not even a good bye? I was so hurt but I don't know why. I should have seen it coming all that talk about needing to start over somewhere else. I should have known she meant her not us. Things were always better when she was gone though. My grandmother came over to stay with us later that week. Things were going really good again. My mom eventually called us about two weeks after she left to let us know she loved us and was ok. My brother wouldn't talk to her by this point them two barely spoke. I spoke to her a couple times a week. As much as I hated her, I couldn't help but dream that one day she would be okay and that she would beat this alcoholism and we could focus on being a family.

She mailed me a letter about a month after she left wrapped in the letter was a plane ticket to come stay with her for a while. She said I would love it. That she barely drank down there she felt she was a whole different person. My grandmother begged me not to go but I was so young and wanted so much to believe that I would go down there and she would be just like a normal working mother. Then maybe we could come back and be a happy family. Mike said I was crazy but I just had to go. I got on the airplane and flew all by myself to meet her. When I got there, she was waiting for me at the gate. She looked really nice in a suit and had make up on. It seemed like a dream I couldn't help getting very excited and thinking this was it we would now be OK.

Soon after I got there, I realized things were still the same. She drank every night and I would sit with her while she drank. I had no choice I didn't have any friends and I really didn't want to call my grandmother and Mike to tell them how bad it was going so I would just sit and listen to her sad stories and play music. We had some OK times there but what I was looking for wasn't there at all. I did not need or want another friend. I wanted a mother and the closest thing to that I had my grandmother who was now so far away. I called my brother and he said for me to go to her and tell her I wanted to come home. Well I did and boy did the good times stop there she told me I was staying and that was it. If I didn't want to be there that I never would have got on that plane. My grandmother tried to talk to her and convince her it was the best thing for me. She told my grandmother that I need to accept the decision I made and deal with it. She also said they needed to stop babying me so I just had to accept I came here and until she left I would be stuck here. She met a guy and started taking me with her to his house every night for weeks. We would stay there till two or three o'clock in the morning. I was about ten at the time so I would have to fight to stay awake. The guy had a son of his own who was about fifteen at the time. I could tell he felt so bad for me but didn't say a word. My mom would tell me to sit in the room with him while she sat in the basement with her friend. I barely said anything when I was there. I felt so uncomfortable there I just sat and looked at the TV not even watching it just staring trying not to fall asleep. I would go in the basement and ask her if we could please go home that I was tired and just wanted to lie in bed and go to sleep. She told me to go lay on the couch that if I fell asleep she would carry me to the car. I told her I didn't sleep well at strange places and that made her furious. She grabbed me by the arm and took me up stairs and said that I would lay on the couch and that she was not going to let me ruin this for her. She said no one likes a selfish and constant complaining kid and that she would never find someone to love her with two rotten kids like she has. I just shut up and sat on the couch every night till early hours of the morning.

    She got fired a few weeks later and we were finally on our way back home. Things were no better when we got back home though. She drank all the time and of course she found a new boyfriend. He was really nice but I don't know how he ended up with her. He drank a lot also but he stayed pretty level headed most of the time he was drinking unless he drank liquor. He loved her I could tell but when she drinks she will do evil things. He suspected her cheating and they were fighting quite a bit for a while so I tried to spend a lot of my time down the street at my friends' house. It was Thanksgiving and she cooked a big dinner. We ate early around two thirty or so. I left after dinner to go to my friends for a while. They were getting pretty drunk off the wine at dinner and I could tell things were starting to heat up.

    I got home around eight o'clock that night and I don't know what happened while I was gone but the whole house was trashed I had two ten-gallon fish tanks and they were kicked in and all my fish were all over the floor. My dog was hiding under the table. The turkey dinner and all the plates were smashed all over the floor. All the pictures were off the walls broke. I wasn't quite sure what to do I was stunned and so upset I just had to get out of there but it was pretty late and most of my friends had bedtimes and that sort of thing so I couldn't go to their houses. I called my brother at his girlfriend's house to tell him what happened. He drove over and came and got me. We stayed at her house for the rest of the night. When we got home the next morning we found out my mom had dumped her boyfriend and the house was the result of his actions. We all chipped in to clean up. I had watched many men come and go over the years but that had to be the worst mess I had ever seen. What kills me is my mom acted as if it was no big deal. Your home is supposed to be your security zone that makes you feel safe. My house on the other hand could turn into a war zone at any time. We were always keeping alert because living with my mother you never know what's going to happen next.

We were having some tough times over the next year but me and my brother just took it day by day. I could tell he was really ready to get his own place but I think he stayed so I wouldn't have to be in that mess alone. One day we had all been fighting with each other pretty bad and I could see in her eyes something bad was going to happen. You never knew with her what it was going to be next. She said Charlie was costing her too much money and she was sick and tired of the dog hair around the house. Not that she was ever there but she knew we loved that dog more than anything. That dog spent so many nights with me when no one was home so to me he was my best friend. She called me and my brother down stairs and said we had to go outside and get Charlie ready that he was leaving. I cried and begged her to please not get rid of my dog. She didn't even care and told me to move it. I'll never forget that day. It was a sunny spring day we got Charlie on a leash and asked her where he was going and she said just put him in the car and get in. I said to her to please not to do this. He doesn't belong in the pound. He is my best friend. She replied so calmly that he wasn't going to the pound. She was taking him for a long ride near the state park a half hour from our house and was going to dump him out. I was devastated!

We got to a wooded road near the park and she pulled the car over. My heart was pounding. Would anyone find him to help him? She opened the door and told us to let him out. I hugged him so tight and told him I was so sorry and that I loved him very much. At first he sniffed around thinking it was a bathroom break. Then she started pulling away and I screamed. He heard me and came running she drove faster and faster he could not run fast enough to catch our car. He ran after our car for about a mile or so. I looked out that back window watching him run. I will never forget watching him run after the car that image I will carry with me for the rest of my life. I would never forgive her for that. Me and my brother sat in the back of that car and never said a word. I always tried to not let my mother see me cry but this day I just couldn't stop. He was gone and I couldn't stop her I felt so guilty Charlie would have died for me and I let this happen to him. I wasn't even sure why she did this was it something I had done? I knew I would never be the same after that day I was heart broken and had no power to stop her. How could she do this to me? She said he will be fine. He is a strong dog. I had nightmares for weeks after that. I could see him running after us in my dreams. I will never forget him.

# *Chapter Three*

After the incident with Charlie I became very withdrawn from her and life all together. I only spoke around her if she made me answer one of her off the wall questions. That made her furious because she would get drunk and try to be my friend and try to get me to hug her and act like she was the funniest, best mom around. I shrugged every hug off and asked if I could go to bed. I kept a picture of Charlie under my pillow and prayed every night that he was OK. My mother didn't like me spending so much time in my room she said it was ridiculous the way I sulked over that stupid dog. She would always bust in my room drunk and go on about how weak of a person I was. The one night she came in and saw me shove Charlies picture under my bed. She walked over and took the picture out and said is this what you do up hear all day and night cry over this picture? Well not anymore and she ripped the picture up in tiny pieces I jumped up and asked her please no but she didn't even hesitate. My hate for her grew so strong after that and they say what doesn't kill you will make you stronger and that day it became very apparent me that I would have to some how get the strength to stand up to her. Over the next year I really started maturing and figuring her out. I just turned thirteen and I was no longer afraid of her. She would come home from long nights out and I would tell her she made me sick. I couldn't hold back any longer. She came home from one of her long nights and me, and my brother and one of his friends were still awake in Mikes room. She came in and said she was in a bar fight that night.

She said she kicked some lady's ass. She told me to stand up and tried to demonstrate on me to show off in front of my brother's friend. She started swinging at me and hit me in the eye. I don't know what happened inside of me but I just lost it. I went after her. My brother and his friend broke us up. Mike carried her in her room and told her not to come back out. I was so embarrassed yet still so furious.

The next morning I woke up with a black eye and she acted like nothing had happened. I told everyone in school I got in a fight with another girl. How could I say my mom and me were fist fighting? No one questioned it though because in my school fighting was like a sport. Over the next couple of months every time we got into an argument she threw her fists up. My brother was not always there to break us up so some got bad. She always usually got the best of me but one afternoon she was so drunk and she came at me and I finally got the best of her. She left running out of the house bleeding and was yelling I better be gone when she got back. She always said that though so I thought nothing of it. I was sitting in the chair in the kitchen cleaning my cuts up when the phone rang. It was my grandmother she said my mom had called my dad and said if he didn't come get me I would be on the streets tonight. I didn't want to go live with him. I barely spoke to him.

My grandmother said he would be expecting me. He lived about ten minutes away so she told me to pack up what I could carry there and Mike would get the rest for me. I called one of my cousins who lived near by and asked her if she would mind helping me carry a couple of bags to my dad's house. She came right away and we carried four bags to my dad's house. That was the last time I got to see the inside of that house. I lived there thirteen years and had left in a matter of minutes. I felt so unsure of everything. Is she really sending me here? As bad as it was at home, it was ok most of the time she wasn't there. Sure I didn't like being alone but when Mike was there we were a family just the two of us. I would miss him more then anything. My mother never called me and Mike brought the rest of my stuff and told me that he was getting his own apartment. He said I could come over whenever I wanted but it still would never be the same.

Staying at my dad's wasn't so bad it just never felt comfortable like home. I felt like I didn't belong there. My heart was so beaten and battered by this point I wasn't sure if I belonged anywhere. I stopped doing my work at school I just didn't feel like it I handed tests in with just my name on the top. I sat through every class with my head down on the desk. I got straight F's for the whole fourth marking period. I still managed to pass eighth grade though because I had straight A's the first three marking periods. My teachers tried to talk to me but I would play it off and give them the I just don't feel like doing it excuse. My dad was furious. He yelled and screamed but I don't think I heard a word. It didn't matter to me. I honestly didn't care what he had to say. He didn't know me or what I was going through or what I've been through. When I said that to him he just got quiet and said go ahead ruin your life then. I said OK and went to my room. As far as I was concerned my life was ruined the day it started and that was the reality of this whole situation.

That whole summer I didn't speak to my mom at all. For some odd reason it really bothered me she wasn't calling. I thought about her often. I started staying out till late at night all summer. I just didn't like sitting at my dad's house. It felt so uncomfortable. I could tell he expected me to be this normal happy kid not this bitter and battered sole. My friends soon became my new family. I would stay over someones house just about every night of the week. My dad didn't mind I think he felt just as uncomfortable around me as I did around him. It's not that he didn't love me it's just I only saw him every other weekend. He didn't know my friend's names or what I did. All of a sudden he has a thirteen-year-old daughter to control. It was too much for both of us I just kept him posted on where I was by phone calls. I checked by phone twice a day just to let him know where I was and where I was staying.

My friends and I started drinking and smoking pot that summer. God it felt so good just to smoke a joint and laugh with my friends. But no matter how messed up I got, I carried my burden of sadness with me. I wanted so badly just to be home in my own bedroom again. I had been sleeping on other people's floors for over a month now. I went to my dad's a couple of times a week to pick up money that he would leave at the house for me. The one day I stopped in and saw an envelope on the counter addressed to me. It was a letter from my mother I could tell instantly by the handwriting. In it she wrote how she was sorry it had to be this way that her life was pretty upside down right now and that she would be moving with her new boyfriend in a couple weeks. She asked if I would call her. She said she would like to take me out on her new boyfriend's boat with a couple of her friends. Of course I called her immediately and I don't know why. She told me she was going to pick me up in a few days. She said it would be a lot of fun. I went to Mike's apartment which wasn't far from my dad's and told him. He said for me just to be careful because I know how she likes to show off in front of her friends after she gets drunk. He told me I should have only agreed to go if they didn't drink. I told Mike not to worry that I could handle her but that didn't seem to give him any comfort.

She picked me up about nine o'clock that morning. It was really weird but I was excited to see her. We had breakfast alone and met up with her new boyfriend and two of their friends after. They seemed really nice. We drove to the dock where he kept his boat. We all loaded in and started cruising. It was all right for a couple of hours until they all started getting really drunk. They all decided we would anchor the boat near this island and we would get out and swim to the island. I told them I had new clothes on my dad had just bought me and that I didn't want to get in the water. My mom new I didn't like getting in water that had things living in it anyway. The comment I made about the clothes my dad bought me kind of pissed her off right away. Her and her friends started calling me a party pooper and my mom asked me why I always had to ruin a good time. This went on for about fifteen minutes until they decided they were just going to leave me in the boat alone.

They went over to the island and took all the sodas and food with them. I sat in the hot sun on the boat for about an hour until I was so sun burned and thirsty I had to yell over if she would please bring me a drink. She said I would have to come get a drink myself. I started crying because I was so frustrated. Why would she bring me out here if all she wanted to do was drink with her friends? About a half an hour went by and her boyfriend came swimming over to the boat. She was yelling you better leave her alone she's a bitch. He offered to carry me on his shoulders over to the island to get some food and something to drink and to get me out of the sun before I passed out. I agreed I had no other options at this point. When I got to the island she threw a soda and a sandwich at me and told me to go sit alone that I was an ungrateful bitch and she didn't want me to ruin her and her friend's good time. I went and sat on a tree log in the shade and ate my sandwich.

I sat there for about two hours before they were ready to go. I walked over to her boyfriend and asked if he could help me back to the boat. He said sure but I know she wasn't happy about it she turned around and gave us the dirtiest look. He said just give her a break she just wants to go home. When I got back in the boat her and her friends were talking about me as if I wasn't even there. So I finally said I just want to go home I have had a long day and I didn't want to argue with anyone. She got so mad and started on me about not wanting to get wet again. I told her it was a mistake for me to come. She got so mad she flew from the other side of the boat and said I'm going to throw you in that water. We wrestled for a bit till her boyfriend broke us up. Her girlfriend was yelling let her go she's gonna teach that girl a lesson. She handed my mom this big float type of thing and whispered for her to throw it at me that it would knock me in the water. She tried too but because I heard them I was able to move out of the way. Her boyfriend sat next to me the rest of the ride and boy did that piss her off. Nothing made her madder then someone sticking up for me. It has always been as if she has been jealous of me.

When we got back to the dock, she told me to get off the boat. I climbed out and stood on the dock and asked if she was going to drive me back home. She said your dad is such a hero call him to come get you and she drove off in the boat with her friends. I had no idea where I was. I had no money and even if I did my dad was at work and I didn't tell him I was coming to meet her. He would have never agreed with that. I sat on the side of the dock and started crying. A really nice man and his wife came over and asked me if I needed any help. I asked them if they could tell me what town I was in and if they had a quarter for the pay phone. They gave me all the change in their pockets and I walked to the pay phone. I only had two quarters for the phone so I called my grandmother and told her where I was and what had happened. She said to give her fifteen minutes and she would call around to find someone to come and get me. I called her back with my last quarter and she said Mike was home and he was on his way to get me. When he got there, I was so glad to see him. We drove home and I just sat so quiet I think Mike could tell I was really counting on that to be a good day with my mom.

The rest of the summer I didn't hear from her at all. I had heard my grandmother talking to someone saying that she had moved two hours away. She didn't even call me to say good bye. I spent the rest of my summer partying with my friends staying at their houses. I guess my dad had called my grandmother about what we were going to do about sending me to high school. He said he didn't think it was a good idea for me to go to the local high school that it was really bad there and he thought it would be good for me to get out of that area for a while. They decided to send me to live with my Aunt who lived in a good school district. I wanted to stay in my school with all my friends. I even asked if they would mind if I dropped out. They didn't go for that one. I just didn't want to move again. My Aunt is really nice and she has two daughters of her own but I hate the unstable feeling that moving from house to house gave me. It was such a empty cold feeling.

## Chapter Four

I moved in with my Aunt a couple of days before school started. I kept my stuff in trash bags in my cousin's room and slept on the floor. Basically your typical handout. I was so used to taking care of myself that I hated the idea of having to be home at a certain time for dinner and having a time I had to be in at night. The school was so different from the school I went to. Everyone had on Polo shirts and khakis and mostly everyone was white. In my last school I was one of the four white people in the class. These people were really snobby and had these happy little home lives. Going shopping with mom after school and seeing a movie with dad that night. I mean give me a break I definitely didn't fit in here. I ended up making friends with the stoners who cut class and hung out behind the football field all day. I went to my grandmothers every weekend and hung out with my old friends. I really missed the privacy of my own bedroom though I got so tired of carrying a bag of clothes everywhere I went. Sometimes I would just go in my grandmother's bathroom and lock the door and just write or draw for hours. A lot of my belongings like stuff I made when I was in grade school kind of just got lost from me moving from one place to the other. Nobody had room for me and all my belongings so I had to keep just what I needed like clothes and shoes.

By the time the first quarter of school was over I had managed to fail every class I had. My Aunt said I would be grounded for weeks. I had never been grounded before and didn't realize just how boring it was. There are a lot of hours in a day to fill. I have never been the type of person to just sit around. Even if I am just drawing, I like to be outdoors and you can only draw so much. And when you don't have a bedroom to escape in its really frustrating. I started skipping school even more so I could hang out during the day because all night I would be sitting on my Aunts couch watching whatever it was they were watching on tv because getting the remote was never an option. I felt so out of place but I really didn't have any other place to go so I guess I would just have to learn to adjust. The feeling you have when you have no where to stay is so weird. It's like if you were running down an alley and you hit a brick wall and you know there is no way your getting over it. No matter what you do or how hard you try so you just have to sit and except the fact that you may never get over that wall. I just had to accept the fact home was no longer there. I would have to keep my head up and just go where there was room for me to stay and be grateful I had somewhere to stay.

One morning before school started I was out back of the football field getting high and I smoked more then usually that day. I went into first period and the teacher must have smelled it because two seconds after I sat down she walked over and told me to go to the nurse. I really wasn't sure what was going on at that point but I did what she asked and headed for the nurse's office. When I got there the dean was standing in there waiting for me. The teacher must have called him to meet me there. He and the nurse asked me to step in one of the exam rooms. They shut the lights out and I asked what was going on and they started flashing a flash light in my eyes saying my pupils wouldn't dilate. I was so nervous and paranoid that my mind went blank and I just said the first thing that came to my mind. I told them they were broke and never worked. They looked at me like I had a third arm coming out of my head and told me to lay down they knew I was on drugs and they were calling my grandmother. So I laid on the cot and waited for my grandmother to get there. I wasn't even scared that she was coming I was more upset that she would have to sit there and listen to them tell her I was on drugs. She was the only person who believed in me and I knew this would really let her down.

My grandmother was not happy to hear what they had to say but she seemed as though she was not surprised. She came in and we had a meeting with the dean and he told my grandmother that when a student is caught under the influence on school property that the school required you to go through a two week live in drug program. I flipped I did not want to go stay at some rehab for two weeks there was no way! They sent me home with her so we could discuss what we were going to do. I would not be allowed on school property until I finished the course. My grandmother thought it would be a good idea for me to go to the rehab but I refused. My grandmother was really good about hearing me out and being supportive on what I thought. She knew I basically raised myself all those years so she knew I was very strong minded. My father on the other hand kind of flipped out but was up in arms on what to do. Plus how could he sit and lecture me about something he does himself. I think everyone was just ready to give up on me. I took the next couple of days to stay with my grandmother and figure out what to do. My dad said there was no way he would agree to signing me out of school for good. He said he would rather admit me to a job core type of training program. That I didn't want either.

I couldn't help over the next couple of days thinking about where my mother was and that maybe she could help me. I was probably crazy for even thinking of that but I was kind of blocked in a corner. I called one of her friends from the neighborhood and they gave me her phone number. I told my grandmother I was going to call her and we fought for about an hour until I just walked out of the house and said I was going to do what I want. I went to my friend's house who lived on the street I lived on with my mom. Her mom always told me I was always welcome there. I called my mom as soon as I got there. I think I reacted way to fast but what did I know at that age.

After I told my mom what was going on she of course loved drama and wasted no time acting like the hero. She called my grandmother to tell her she was coming to get me to stay with her. My grandmother called my dad who didn't like the idea but didn't know what else to do. He called my school and told them I would be transferring out of the district. They said it would be fine but if I ever wanted to return to the school that I would still have to enter the rehab.

My mom was there to get me two days later. On the long ride to her new house we talked a lot. She seemed to be doing all right. She said she has a new job and that it is really quiet where her apartment is. She said it was in the country on a back road and it was a duplex and she had one really nice neighbor. She said there was a stream in her back yard with miles of wooded trails. When we got to her apartment, I was surprised it was really cute. She actually kept it clean and had food in the refrigerator. Not like the last house we lived together in. I enrolled in the school there and boy was that an even bigger change then before. The school was so small about ten kids in a class. I was definitely going to need some time to get used to living in the mountains. Over the next couple of weeks things were pretty good with my mom. She still drank but seemed to be on a happy streak or something. Maybe it was the new boyfriend or something whatever it was I wasn't going to complain. I did miss my friends and family though. This was the first time I was too far to just go and visit them.

After being there a month and having some time to think I realized this was not where I wanted to be. I realized running from my problems was just the easy way out. I really wanted to go home but I didn't know how to tell my mom that. She was acting so proud of herself for rescuing me from what she called one of those brain washing institutes. I waited till she was in one of her really happy drunk moods and I told her it was really great seeing her and not arguing all the time. But I really wanted to go back to my old school and go through the program. She didn't take it well at all. I shouldn't have been surprised but I guess I thought since things were going pretty well and she was treating me like an adult that she would see I was trying to do what I thought was best for me right now. But instead she called me a trader and said my dad was probably behind this. She started packing my stuff and throwing things at me. I was getting really scared because I was two hours from anyone I knew that could come get me. I went in the other room and called my grandmother and told her what was happening. My mom saw me on the phone and ran over and grabbed me by the hair and started punching me in the head. I finally got her pinned down and kept asking her are you done? Finally she said yes so I let her up she turned around and spit at me and told me to be out of her house by tomorrow that she was going to stay at a friend's house. I called my grandmother back and she said she already called my dad and that he was on his way over to drop his car off to her to come get me. I got packed and about two o'clock in the morning I heard a car pull up and it was my grandmother.

I can't even explain how good it felt to see her. We drove back through the night and didn't say much. I have to say I was a little disappointed things had to end in such a bad way with my mom. We were getting along so well even with her daily drinking. When I got back, I agreed to start the program in two weeks. The school year was just about over and I already failed for the year so I would go to the program for two weeks and then have summer vacation and I could start fresh next year. When I got back, I right away called my friends and by that night we had a welcome home party. I took my first hit of acid and I have to say I never laughed so much in my life. I took a hit every day from then on till I had to enter the program. When I got to the rehab I had a bit of change of heart and really didn't want to be there but I knew that this was something I just had to do. They checked me in my room and gave me the run down of the rules the biggest one was I was not allowed to call anyone or have any visitors. They called this blackout for two weeks. I was so pissed after hearing that. I kind of made up my mind right there that I would just be there and that I was not going to participate in anything. The first week went by pretty fast I met a really cool girl who was not from around here. Her parents sent her so far away because she kept sneaking out of every rehab they put her in and went and partied with her friends. Well that made a light bulb go off in my head. That was it I had to come up with a plan.

It only took me one day to find a door that no cameras were at. It was in the back of the work out room. I took one of my shoe boxes and folded it to fit in the door where the latch in the door was which then kept it unlocked for me to get back in. I told my friend there that she was more then welcome to join me. Of course she did and we went out and had the best time with my friends. There was a carnival in town and everyone I knew was there. One of my old friends had PCP with him. Well I had never tried it and he kept bugging me to smoke with him so I agreed. My friend from rehab also had never tried it and wanted to too. After I smoked it, I didn't really like it. I felt like I had moon boots on and I kept lifting my knees to my chest when I was walking. My body felt like a stay puff marshmallow man and my face kept getting numb like when you just get out of the dentist. Who knows I might have even been drooling. It was cool for the night but I definitely didn't want to do it anymore. We got back to the rehab at about three in the morning. We went in the door that I had rigged but one thing I didn't plan on was an alarm going off. The door activated an alarm when it was opened after hours. I heard it go off and I looked at her she was a mess so I told her to hide under a table and when the guards came in I said I was trying to get out to have a cigarette and the alarm went off. I couldn't believe it but they bought it and told me that I was not allowed to smoke after hours. I headed up stairs and when they left I went back down for my friend and helped her get up the steps. We stayed close friends the rest of the time I was there which made my last week there go by fast. We just sat and laughed every day about our crazy night. When I left, we said we wanted to try to stay in touch but both of our lives were so unstable at the time I think we both knew that probably wasn't going to happen. But we were left with one really great night to remember and I'll probably never forget it.

When I got out, I was back to staying at different friends houses. I did that the rest of the summer just kind of floating from one place to the next. I didn't hear from my mom at all that summer but didn't have much time to think about it. I knew school would be here soon and I would really have to try to make it work this time. I think everyone was waiting for me to fail. My Aunt I was staying with called my grandmother and told her she didn't really want me staying with her anymore. I guess I was just too much for anyone to handle. My grandmother sounded pretty disappointed but said she would work something out before school started and I would have a place to stay. You know I really hated being a burden on her but I didn't really have anyone else to turn to. Without her I don't know where I would be.

# *Chapter Five*

School was getting ready to start and my grandmother was still having no luck with anyone taking me in. Finally my other aunt who lived in the district agreed to take me in but I could tell it took much convincing and begging from my grandmother. She also drank every day and dabbled with some drugs and had a daughter five years younger then me. I started school off with a positive outlook I knew how many days I was allowed to be absent before receiving an F. So I would limit and regulate my skipping school. I still partied but I made sure I was in bed at a reasonable time. I called it responsible partying my friends always got a kick out of it when I would say I got to go I am trying to party responsibly. My Aunt was pretty cool and things were going pretty good. All the drinking and partying she did kind of made me feel at home. I started feeling really sick though and I was losing a lot of weight over the next couple of months. I of course just thought it was the drugs so I would wear stretch pants under my jeans when I knew I would be seeing someone in my family. That was the last thing I needed everyone looking at me talking about how skinny I was getting like some freak of nature. You get the look with their head tilted down their eyebrows pressed down and then comes the lean and whisper. I mean don't people know that is not being discreet everyone then knows your talking about me. It's so childish.

    It started getting really bad when I would get really short of breath just walking up a couple of steps. I mean I even knew that this was ridiculous. I went to my grandmother after passing out a few times just hanging with friends. The first time I passed out I was standing around this guys bed with my friends when I passed out and fell face first into the bed. Next thing I know my friend is shaking my shoulder asking what I was doing. When I said what is going on they all said you just flopped in his bed and laid there. I was so embarrassed I told them I think I just passed out but I wasn't sure. The last time I passed out I hit my head on someones coffee table and had the biggest egg on my head. I knew something wasn't right. My grandmother took me to the doctors and they drew some blood after seeing the amount of weight I had lost. It took a week for the results to get back and I just continued as normal. In the back of my mind though I couldn't help but wonder if it was something serious? When the doctor called he said me and my grandmother would have to come in for a visit as soon as possible to talk about the results. I knew this couldn't be good. I was so nervous the day of the appointment I thought for sure he would say it was because of the drugs and I would end up back in some kind of program.

When we got in there he said I had contracted mono some time ago. He said maybe as long as a year or two ago and because I never got much rest and was under constant stress that it never got better. It progressed into something that now was affecting my liver. He said my liver was as hard as a rock and I would have to be very careful just walking around not to fall or it could bust or something. He told me I would not be able to return to school this year that I would have to be home schooled. He said the school would provide me with a home school teacher. I also would have to have blood drawn every other week to keep an eye on it. I couldn't believe it I just started school again and was determined to do good and I get to stay home anyway. I have to admit I was pretty stoked about the whole thing. That is until I was told I would be on complete bed rest until my blood work showed improvements.

I went home and stayed at my grandmothers and she would drive me back and forth to meet the home school teacher once a week at my Aunts because that was my address for school. I got really bored at my grandmothers house fast so I called my really good friend Sam that I grew up with and asked him if I could stay with him and his family. Sam lived ten houses away from me when I lived with my mother. His mom said ok. I was so excited now I just had to convince my grandmother it was a good idea. It was pretty hard to convince her but Sams mom called her and said she would keep an eye on us. She knew my situation with my mom and all. I had always kept in touch with Sam even through all my moving. He was definitely my best friend. Me and Sam just kind of hung out around his house in my old neighborhood. We just smoked pot because I had to give the other drugs up to help get my blood work up. After a month of bed rest I was allowed to walk around for short distances. It was getting really annoying I was fourteen sitting still wasn't my idea of fun but at least my friends were close. Me and Sam became very close over the next few months. He stayed in with me every time I couldn't go somewhere. We talked a lot about how we both wanted to get out of this neighborhood and make something of ourselves. Sam who never got the chance to even go to high school said we probably wouldn't make it due to our backgrounds. Just writing your address on some job applications made people look at you funny like you were a theif. Its like people label you before they even speak to you.

Sam got a job with a construction company in about the middle of the school year which meant I spent a lot of my time alone again. I would just hang around the neighborhood all day until he got home. One afternoon I got a letter at Sams house from my mother. I was very hesitant to read it. I let it sit on Sam's dresser for two days before I opened it. She wrote about how she was living alone again and left her boyfriend. She was staying at a motel about fifteen minutes out of town. She said that writing seemed to be the best way for us to stay in contact now because anytime we try to meet it turns into a big mess. I didn't write her back but I have to admit hearing from her did really feel good. I don't know what it was but there was something about her that I couldn't let go. The letters would come about once a month and she would send checks with them sometimes. I started saving them in a savings account. She would ask in her letters why I did not write back she said she knew I was getting the letters because I was cashing the checks. To tell you the truth I don't know why I didn't write back. I enjoyed her letters I just wasn't sure if I could let go of what has happened. I mean I am fifteen years old now and I haven't had a stable place to live in a few years and I was sad about that but wasn't really sure if putting the blame on any specific person was the right thing to do. I always try to be a fair good caring person and causing someone pain over my little sad story just wasn't my style. I am in control of my life now and until I can prove to everyone I will make something of myself I think keeping to myself is the best idea.

As the school year started coming to an end I was starting to feel a lot better and the doctor told me my blood work was looking good. He said I would be ready for next year in school for sure. When he said that I kind of got scared. That was something I definitely didn't think about with all my spare time. When Sam got home from work we talked about where they might send me to live for school. I had gotten really comfortable living at Sams and though it wasn't home. It felt great being in the comfort zone of my old neighborhood. And reality was I didn't have a home anymore and that was something I had to face. Me and Sam came up with this great plan that we could get a apartment with all the money we saved. The only problem with that was neither of us were eighteen. Sam would turn eighteen in the middle of next school year but that didn't help me now. I had to convince my grandmother to let me stay at Sams while I went back to school. I told her I was sick of moving around and that I could get a part time job and could pay her for all the gas she used to take me and pick me up. She said she would think about it. That really meant if I cant find somewhere else for you it would have to be OK. So that summer I decided I would look for a job. I got hired at a dry cleaners. I mean it wasn't the most fabulous job but with them paychecks and the checks coming from my mom I really managed to save quite a bit of money. At a time when most of my friends were spending all their money on getting high and having fun I spent most of my time dreaming of a place to call home.

I would sit at some of the parties and just look around and laugh at them being so messed up and I tell you from a outside straight point of view some of them were beginning to look a mess. That made me wonder is that what I looked like all messed up? I was always the type of person who liked to look good even if things wernt going so good but when you are high they are the type of things I guess you kind of let go. I am definitely a firm believer of "you are the company you keep". I knew something had to change but these were my friends. I think Sam was the only one who would actually think outside the box with me. Sometimes we would go to the woods I sat in as a kid and roll up a joint of pot and just laugh and talk for hours. Sitting there sometimes made me think of Charlie and how much I missed him. I would always talk about getting older and helping abandoned animals just like Charlie whose owners (my mother) just threw him out of a car and left him to fend for his self.

## Chapter Six

Summer came and went before I knew it and school was just two weeks away and my grandmother still didn't tell me if it was OK to stay at Sams. I called her to talk to her about it and she said my dad wasn't crazy about the idea but said it would be fine if she thought it was the right thing to do. So with some major begging she allowed me to stay. Me and Sam were stoked!! We had become best friends through all of this. I started school like any other year but actually had something to work at this year. If my grades went down I would have to stay at my grandmothers sleeping in a sleeping bag on the living room floor. So I actually made an effort to make it to class this time. At least the important ones. I knew I could miss nine days of every class each marking period without getting a automatic F. I had it down to a science. I would skip one class in the morning to have breakfast at the little diner down the street. I was in there so much that they made a student special for me because I complained that there was all these senior citizens specials and no specials for the students. So they made a student special for me with my favorite breakfast two dippy eggs with toast and a soda. In the afternoon I would pick a class to skip also so I could meet with my friends behind the football field to smoke a joint. The first time I went back there from being on home school I was suprised to see last years freshman kids that started coming down behind the field made a vine swing over the creek. Well of course I had to try it. The thing was I hadn't built up that much muscle in my arms from being sick so when I got out over the creek I fell straight down like a ton of bricks. It was freaking hysterical. You should have seen me trying to explain to my teachers why I was soaking wet and covered in mud. They didn't find it as funny as I did and I got detention but I think in my opinion it was definitely worth it.

Sam turned eighteen before I knew it and we were secretly apartment hunting. I don't know why I was so secretive about it but I really didn't want anyone to know. I guess I didn't want to hear anyones negative comments about how young we were and that we would probably fail plus I was still just fifteen getting ready to turn sixteen in a few months. Any one of my parents could object to this and make me stay somewhere else. We found this really cute apartment about five minutes up the street from Sams house. The landlord said he could not put me on the lease because I was not eighteen but I was OK with that because I trusted Sam. I knew if anyone he would not put me on the streets. I was so excited when the day came to move we told Sams mom to please not tell anyone that called for me that we got our own place to just call me and I would call them right back. She did she was so excited for us. We got the key and me and Sam just laid on the empty living room floor and just smiled. I couldn't believe it my own home. I felt like I waited an eternity for this. It was very hard with the school thing though I had to get up an hour early so I could walk to meet my grandmother at Sams house where she picked me up for school. She would drop me off at work and then pick me up after and drive me back to Sams house. Then after going to school all day and working all night I had to walk to my apartment. This went on for months I was getting so drained from all the covering up that I slept any spare time I could get away.

After having my own place for a few months I had this humble feeling about myself. I actually accomplished something and the funny thing was I couldn't even brag about it to all those people that most likely would of doubted me. I kept getting the letters from my mother and I really wanted to start writing back and I would sit at my kitchen table for hours thinking of what to write but didn't even know where to begin and if I did finish a letter it would sit for days in a envelope and then I would throw it away. I think I really just wanted to scream at her and ask her why she did this to me and Mike all these years. I wanted so bad to be able to rub in her face about my nice place and show her I no longer needed her or anyone for that matter. But because I didn't want to jeopardize anything I just kept receiving the letters and not giving any reply. I thought about her often and tried to see things from her point of view. After seeing a lot of my friends going down hill I thought maybe that's what happened to her? I know she loved us but I just don't think she had control of her life enough to actually take care of us. Love and responsibility are definitely not the same thing. I know she came from a hard background and was a hurt sole and just kept allowing her life to spiral out of control. But I could not allow her back in my life right now to ruin what I worked so hard to get. She is definitely not trust worthy or dependable.

My sixteenth birthday came and I figured it would come and go without me even noticing like every other year but when I got in from school that day Sam was standing in my living room with these big three balloons. As I stood in the doorway I heard this little noise and behind him tied to these great big balloons was a little black puppy. I just started crying and Sam looked at me like he was sorry. He said I didn't mean to make you upset I thought this gift out for a while and thought this was the perfect one. I told him to shut up and bring that cute little guy over to me right now. Sam said he met someone on the job that had puppies and they were going to put this one down because he got stuck under the shed for a week and was infested with fleas and they ate a whole through his leg. He had a pretty big wound on half of his leg but the vet said that leg would heal but probably not grow hair ever. Sam knew all I talked about was one day using my pain to help unfortunate animals with theirs. This was the best gift ever!! That night I sat with my little deformed puppy and thought about where my life would be without Sam. We worked as a team to overcome the struggles of growing up in a very poor project. Without him all of this would be so lonely. I knew then I had to tell Sam how I thought. I went in his room were he was sleeping and just crawled in bed next to him and told him I loved him. He said he always loved me from day one but didn't want to take a chance ruining the friendship we found in each other until I was ready. I knew right then that I wanted to be with him the rest of my life. In him I found my home.

I named the puppy Bubba and that little guy made everyday seem that much greater. Me and Sams relationship grew into something so great. Sam bought me a car a few months later which made it a lot easier to get to school and back. I was actually passing and getting pretty good grades too. But one afternoon at school my guidance counselor called me in her office and said she had some pretty bad news about me graduating next year she said that I had not received any gym credits since I was at the school and because this school year was ending soon that there was no way I could get four gym credits next year. I was really depressed because I had been working so hard this year to make things right. I had Sam and Bubba and really wanted to have a great life with them and I knew I needed an education and diploma to ever get a good job. She suggested that after this school year ended to talk to my parents and discuss maybe applying to get my GED. She said I was welcome to attend next year but would definitely not graduate. How was I going to tell my grandmother this she worked so hard to get me here and back everyday that I feel like I am letting her down. She was the one person to always stand behind me.

I finished the school year without mentioning this to anyone I didn't even tell Sam he always talked about me graduating and being so proud of me. However in my spare time I was doing research at the school library during study hall to figure out where my life could go. I thought about community college but I could never afford that and I sure couldn't count on my parents for money. I wanted to do something to deal with numbers or money. I was always very business smart I think from growing up in the projects. Living there you could be hustled out of your last buck and not even know it. I took this summer to just relax and figure it out. You know things were just going good and now I have another hurdle to get over go figure!! I enjoyed the summer by taking long walks around the neighborhood and working extra hours. I decided I would apply for this job I saw in the newspaper it said will train the right person to be a vet tech. I drove up there and didn't even think I would get the job. I went on with everything else like normal well when I got a call two weeks later I couldn't believe it. They actually saw something in me and wanted to give me a chance. They said it would be full time and I would be on probation for three months. I was thrilled and was waiting at the door to tell Sam when he got in. Then he said well what are you going to do when the school year comes back around? That was it I had to tell him. After I finished telling him he just looked stunned. He thought it was still important to go for the GED and that maybe I should make an appointment to take it. When I told him I haven't told my grandmother yet he was a little suprised. I always told her everything.

    I called my grandmother and told her what the guidance counselor had said and she freaked!! She made an appointment to see her the first day of school to hear it for herself. I made the appointment anyway for the GED because I knew what the counselor was going to say. I made it for the day after the meeting because I knew when my dad heard he would flip so I figured I could tell him after I found out if I passed the GED. In the meantime I started my new job and really loved it. I was taking blood and assisting with surgery. It really was interesting and I was learning new stuff everyday and Bubba was welcome to join me at work. The day of the meeting my grandmother looked more hurt then mad after the counselor told her. I guess she was hoping for a miracle that this just wasn't true. The following day she drove with me to take the test. To my surprise I flew right through it. I got the results back two weeks later but they would not send the actual GED until I turned eighteen which was a little over a year away. But at least I still had that letter that said I passed. I stayed with my job as a vet tech and was working about fifty hours a week. I could of stayed there a hundred hours a week I loved that place. I was really comfortable with my life and proud of where I was even if everyone thought I was a loser for dropping out of school. No one still knew I had my own place so to everyone in my family it looked as though I dropped out of school and was staying with Sams mom and doing nothing with my life.

# Chapter Seven

After my seventeenth birthday I realized it was about time I told my grandmother the truth about where I was living and what has been going on in my life. I knew I could trust her she would listen to my feelings and take me serious as an adult. When I told her she seemed really proud of me. It kind of made me wonder why I didn't tell her sooner. She came over and met Bubba and had dinner with me and Sam. She said that if anyone finds out in the family she would take care of it. She raised me since I was little and if she was OK with it then they would have to be OK with it. She told me to never hide your accomplishments in life to always hold your head up and be proud of the decisions you make. She also said my place was really nice and the dog was a little goofy with that odd leg but really nice. I was so happy I didn't have to hide where I lived anymore and worry about one of my goofy parents trying to get me to move out. My grandmother called me about a week later to let me know she told my dad. He didn't take it very well but after fighting with my grandmother on the phone for an hour he came to terms with the whole situation. When I went to visit him a few days later lets just say I could tell he was definitely holding back what he really wanted to say. We had a family barbecue and everyone actually seemed pretty excited for me they wanted to come over and visit. I took Bubba to the barbecue and as always he was a big hit I mean how could you not pity that cute face with that goofy leg. I think he loved all the attention with the leg thing it was almost as if he would walk up to someone and stick his bad leg out as if to say have you seen the leg? He made me smile everyday.

    The next thing I really wanted to do was make amends with my mother. I wanted to let her know that I was living in my own place and had control of my own life. I was hoping we could at least try to be friends and maybe her seeing that she no longer had complete control of me and that I started my own life maybe she could respect me as a woman and a individual. I would be willing to accept her for all the decisions that she has made. Although some of them I probably will never understand. But holding a grudge was definitely not what I wanted to do. I loved my mother and I knew I wanted some kind of relationship with her. I mean I don't think I'll ever respect her as a great mother but maybe we could be great friends. I sat that night and started writing her a letter of pure honest feelings letting her know I did care for her but I needed to prove to myself I could make it in this world before I came to terms with our relationship. I wrote all night about seven pages worth you would think I was writing a book. I told Sam to mail it for me in the morning on the way to work so I wouldn't chicken out and not send it. I heard him leave the next morning and I jumped out of bed to see if he took the letter and of course he did. A couple of days went by and I kind of put the letter in the back of my mind but was still wondering if she got it and what she thought of it.

    About two weeks went by and no letter came. I was a little hurt but didn't resent her at all for taking her time responding I mean it was seven pages there was a lot to take in and think about. It was a Saturday night and me Sam and Bubba just got in from a night visiting with my grandmother. We put in a movie and sat on the couch when my phone rang. It was my grandmother she said my mother had been in a really bad car accident and had passed away on the way to the hospital. I was devastated. I just dropped to the floor crying. I couldn't help but think about all those opportunities I had to write her back and talk to her. They were all gone now. I needed her. I laid in bed and never wanted to get out I just couldn't accept this was happening. The next morning Sam came in from walking Bubba and he brought the mail from yesterday. He reached over the bed and in his hands I saw a letter. I knew right away it was my mother's handwriting. I wasn't really sure if I wanted to open it but I did. The letter said : *Dear Alex I was so excited to get your letter. I didn't know how to answer all the questions you asked me but I am very grateful for your forgiveness. My life wasn't very easy growing up either and when your father left us I back spiraled into this whole of depression. My drinking caused you and Mike so much pain but I was in so deep I felt I could never get out. I wasn't really aware of how every bad decision I made for me would affect you and Mike so much. I love you's both so much but I am not sure what a good mother is. I have never had one either. I hope we can build a friendship on that common ground if any. I am so sorry for all the things you went through and all the emptiness I have caused. I am so glad to here about your place and I am so proud of you. You have accomplished more in your short time of life then I probably ever will. All my problems have made you grow up so fast. You are still just a child and live life as an adult. You give me hope that my life is not such a waste. That you can get whatever you want out of life if your determined. Maybe your pain in life is what keeps you so focused. I am entering a program next week and will not be able to keep in contact with you until I am finished. It is a very intense program that requires no outside contact for a month. Your letter really helped me see the clear picture. I can not go on being like this forever. I contacted someone and got the information on the program and didn't want to write you until I knew I was accepted. I am hoping for someday to be able to make you and Mike proud of me. I love you and will contact you as soon as I can I love You's both Love Always Mom.*

 The doctors said she was going to enter the program the following day that she died. They said she was drinking and driving when she crashed. She must have been out partying her last night before entering the program. They say she fell asleep or passed out at the wheel and drove right into a tree. She died minutes after getting her out of the car. It seemed so unfair. She was finally going to try to be a good mother. I had waited for this my whole life and now it's gone. After the funeral I withdrew from everyone and starting spending a lot of time alone. I would find myself just wandering with Bubba and I always managed to end up sitting on that tree in the woods that over looked our old house. I just stared at the kitchen window kind of hoping just to see her walk by. I'll never know why my mother did the things she did or why her life ended so soon but the one thing I do know is that without all the bumps in the road she created for me my legs would never be this strong to walk through life as I do. A strong independent woman. I know I will carry her in my heart forever and will never look down on her for any the many bad decisions she has made. She had a tough road to walk in life also and I can respect that not everyone has the strength or guidance to make it through. Having my grandmother gave me that extra helping hand I needed to get over my toughest hurdles in life and for that I will always love and respect her. I can now see how easy it is to lose focus and how easily some people just give up on you.

    Me and Sam spent the next few years saving money and we bought our first house. It was great it was a single with a huge yard. We completely renovated the whole house ourselves. We loved fixing it so much that when we were done we then started buying homes to fix up and rent out. After a few years we saved some money and purchased our own farm. We have filled our land with many rescued animals. It is so great to just look out my window and know that this is all mine. I waited so long and worked so hard for all of this. I still find myself thinking of my mother and what it would be like if she was still here. A few months ago I even went back to the spot I always sat with Charlie on the tree that over looked the old house. When I got there though I immediately noticed that they had knocked all the old houses down and built new ones. It was so weird to see my old house gone. Me and Bubba sat there the rest of the afternoon. I just kept staring over just trying to remember the way it once was. I don't think I will ever go back there though. What I once loved there is now gone. Me and Mike are still very close and talk all the time. Mike is married now and has a few kids so I babysit a lot and I love it. My grandmother is good but getting older and don't get around so good anymore. I take her food and coffee just about everyday and we sit and talk for hours. I wish my mother could of been here to grow older with us but she chose her path in life and now we must live with her decision. But she will always be in my thoughts and in my heart.

## THE END

0-595-34988-9

Printed in the United Kingdom
by Lightning Source UK Ltd.
124949UK00001B/344/A